DISCARDED

For my mother

First published in the United States and Canada in 2014 by Lemniscaat USA LLC • New York
Distributed in the United States by Lemniscaat USA LLC • New York

van Hout, Mies
Twinkle, Twinkle, Little Star / Mies van Hout
With audio CD.
1. Children's Songs -- United States 2. Nursery Rhymes

PZ8.3 [E]

ISBN 978-1-935954-37-8 (Hardcover)
Printed in the United States by Worzalla, Stevens Point, Wisconsin

www.lemniscaatusa.com

Mies van Hout

Twinkle, Twinkle, Little Star

lemniscaat

Old MacDonald had a farm, E I E I O,
And on his farm he had some chicks, E I E I O.
With a chick chick here and a chick chick there,
Here a chick, there a chick, everywhere a chick chick.
Old MacDonald had a farm, E I E I O.

Swan swam over the sea,
    Swim, swan, swim!
Swan swam back again,
Well swum, swan!

If you're happy and you know it, clap your hands! (clap clap)

If you're happy and you know it, clap your hands! (clap clap)

If you're happy and you know it, then your face will surely show it!

If you're happy and you know it, clap your hands! (clap clap)

Twinkle, twinkle, little star,

How I wonder what you are!

Up above the world so high,

Like a diamond in the sky.

Twinkle, twinkle, little star,

How I wonder what you are!

I'm a little teapot,
Short and stout.
Here is my handle,
Here is my spout.
When I get all steamed up,
Hear me shout:
"Tip me over,
And pour me out!"

Five little ducks went out one day

Over the hill and far away

Mother Duck said "Quack, Quack, Quack, Quack"

But only four little ducks came back.

Four little ducks (repeat), Three little ducks,
(repeat), Two little ducks (repeat)

No little ducks went out one day
Over the hill and far away
Mother duck said, "Quack, quack, quack, quack,"
and all five ducks came waddling back.

My hat, it has three corners,
Three corners has my hat,
And had it not three corners,
It would not be my hat.

It's raining, it's pouring,

The old man is snoring.

He went to bed and he

Bumped his head

And he couldn't get up in the morning.

If you go down to the woods today

You're sure of a big surprise.

If you go down to the woods today

You'd better go in disguise.

For every bear that ever there was

Will gather there for certain, because

Today's the day the teddy bears have their picnic.

Head and shoulders, knees
and toes, knees and toes,

Head and shoulders, knees
and toes, knees and toes,

And eyes and ears
and mouth and nose.

Head and shoulders, knees
and toes, knees and toes.

The wheels on the bus
go round and round.
round and round.
round and round.

The wheels on the bus
go round and round,
all through the town!

Down by the station early in the morning,

See the little puffer bellies all in a row.

See the engine driver pull the little handle,

Puff, puff! Toot! Toot!

Off we go.